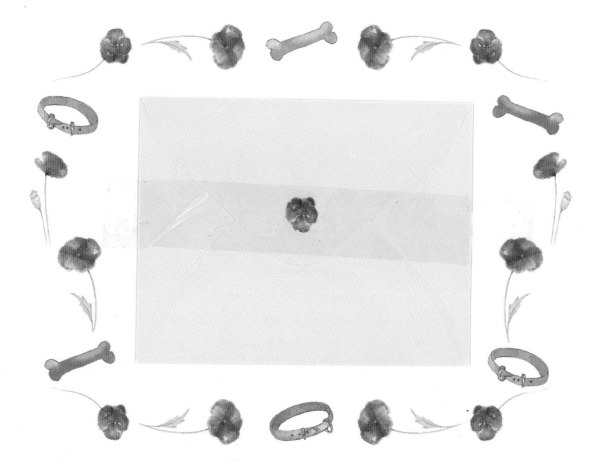

Honeypot Hill

Saffron Thimble's Sewing Shop

← To the City

The Orchards

Paddle Steamer Quay

Aunt Marigold's General Store

Lavender Valley Garden Centre

Healing House and Garden

The Worthingtons' House

Melody Maker's Music Shop

Lavender Lake

Lavender Lake School of Dance

Bumble Bee's Teashop

Peppermint Pond

Hedgerows Hotel
Where Mimosa lives

SCHOOL

Rosehip School

Summer Meadow

Christmas Corner

Wildspice Woods

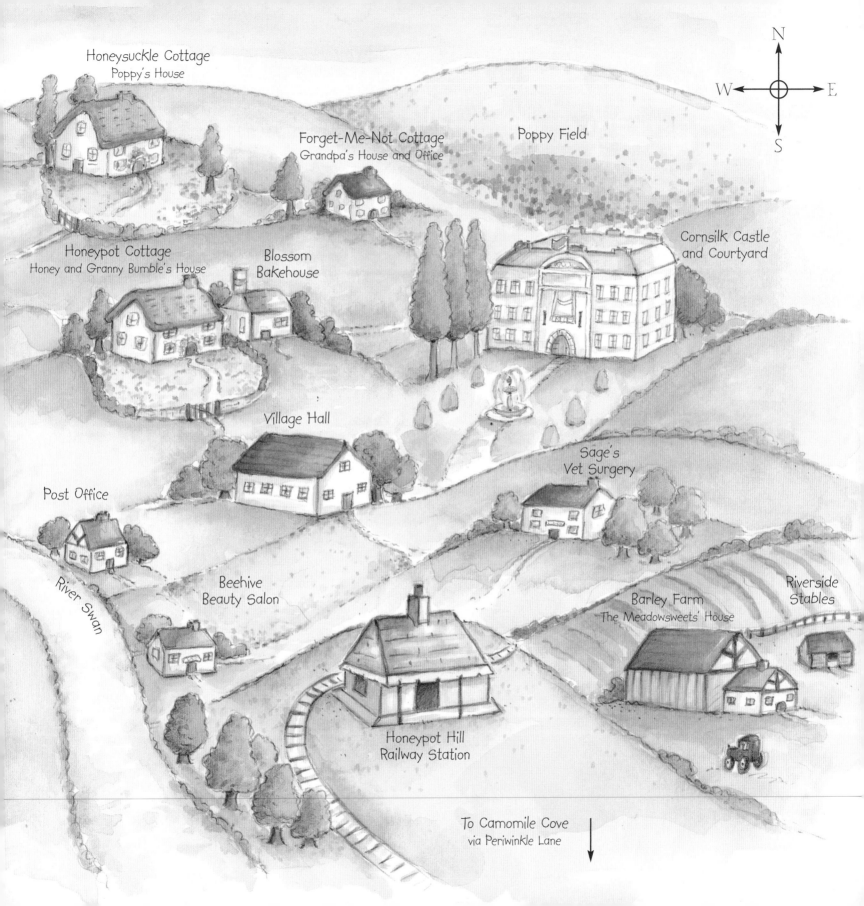

Honeysuckle Cottage
Poppy's House

Forget-Me-Not Cottage
Grandpa's House and Office

Poppy Field

Honeypot Cottage
Honey and Granny Bumble's House

Blossom
Bakehouse

Cornsilk Castle
and Courtyard

Village Hall

Sage's
Vet Surgery

Post Office

Beehive
Beauty Salon

River Swan

Barley Farm
The Meadowsweets' House

Riverside
Stables

Honeypot Hill
Railway Station

To Camomile Cove
via Periwinkle Lane

N
W E
S

Visit Princess Poppy for fun, games, puzzles,
activities, downloads and lots more at

www.princesspoppy.com

★

PUPPY LOVE
A PICTURE CORGI BOOK 978 0 552 56309 3

First published in Great Britain by Picture Corgi,
an imprint of Random House Children's Books
A Random House Group Company

This edition published 2010

3 5 7 9 10 8 6 4 2

Text copyright © Janey Louise Jones, 2010
Illustrations copyright © Picture Corgi Books, 2010
Illustrations by Veronica Vasylenko
Design by Tracey Cunnell

The right of Janey Louise Jones and Veronica Vasylenko to be identified as
the author and illustrator of this work has been asserted in accordance
with the Copyright, Designs and Patents Act 1988.

Picture Corgi Books are published by Random House Children's Books,
61–63 Uxbridge Road, London W5 5SA
www.princesspoppy.com
www.kidsatrandomhouse.co.uk
www.rbooks.co.uk

Addresses for companies within The Random House Group Limited
can be found at: www.randomhouse.co.uk/offices.htm

THE RANDOM HOUSE GROUP Limited Reg. No. 954009

A CIP catalogue record for this book is available from the British Library

Printed in China

Puppy Love

Written by Janey Louise Jones

PICTURE CORGI

For Buddy, a golden bundle of mischief.
And with thanks to Luella Wallace
who taught us puppy love.
★

Puppy Love
featuring

Mum
★

Princess Poppy

Dad
★

Honey
★

Mrs Meadowsweet
★

The puppies
★

"Hi, Poppy," called Honey as she walked up the garden path to Honeysuckle Cottage. "I'm so excited about seeing the puppies at Barley Farm!"

"Me too," replied Poppy. "Let's go!"

"This is going to be the best summer holiday ever!" exclaimed Poppy. She adored puppies and had wanted one for ages. "We'll be able to play with them every day!"

POST OFFICE

OPEN

They found Mrs Meadowsweet in the cosy farmhouse kitchen.
Duchess, the sheepdog, was curled up with
her ten new puppies.

"Aw!" chorused the girls. "They're gorgeous!"

Poppy and Honey visited the puppies every day after that.

Play time!

Nap time!

Tea time!

Chaos in the farmyard!

My favourite!

First slipper!

Growing up fast!

All ten puppies were cute but there was one that Poppy particularly loved. She was the smallest one and always bounded up to Poppy and nuzzled into her as soon as she saw her. Poppy named her Jasmine and secretly hoped that one day she would be hers.

"I wish I could have Jasmine," said Poppy as she and Honey walked home one afternoon.

"That would be amazing," replied Honey. "You should ask your parents."

"I know they'll say no like they did when I asked if I could have a puppy before. They'll say I've got enough pets and that a puppy is too much work," said Poppy glumly.

"If you don't ask, you'll never know," answered Honey.

But Poppy couldn't bear to be disappointed again.

The next day Poppy and Honey went to Barley Farm as usual. They arrived to find Mrs Meadowsweet making 'for sale' adverts for the puppies.

"It's time for them to go to new families," she explained.
"Will you help me and then put them up around the village?"

Poppy could think of nothing worse. She hated the idea of her beloved
Jasmine being sold to another family, but she reluctantly agreed.

When the adverts were finished, the girls set off to put them up.

Poppy was very quiet indeed.

"What's wrong?" Honey asked.

"I'm worried that another family is going to buy Jasmine and I'll never see her again," admitted Poppy tearfully.

"Just ask your mum and dad if you can have her," said Honey. "If you don't try, you'll never know. You *have* to do it!"

Poppy waited until supper time.

"Um, Mum, Dad," she began, "you know the puppies? Um, well, Mrs Meadowsweet is selling them and I, um, wondered whether I could have one."

Mum and Dad looked at one another.

"We've been through this before," said Mum. "I'm sorry, darling, but the answer is no. You have three pets already, hardly any spare time, not to mention the expense and hard work involved in having a dog."

Poppy didn't argue.

The next day, when Poppy and Honey arrived at Barley Farm,
the kitchen was full of people petting the puppies.

When everyone finally left, Mrs Meadowsweet noticed that Poppy wasn't her usual self and asked her what the matter was.

"I asked if Mum and Dad would buy Jasmine but they said no and now she'll go to another family," sobbed Poppy.

"Why don't you take her for a trial day?" suggested Mrs Meadowsweet. "That might just change their minds!"

Poppy ran home to ask right away . . .

Mum and Dad went into the sitting room to discuss it.
Poppy waited nervously in the kitchen.

"We've decided that one day can't hurt," said Dad when
they came back after what seemed like ages.

"Bring her here tomorrow and we'll see," continued Mum.
"No promises though."

"Yippee!" cried Poppy. "I *know* you'll love her!"

Poppy and Honey went to collect the puppy early the next morning.

"Please be good, Jasmine!" Poppy whispered into the lively little pup's ear as they arrived home.

As soon as Poppy, Honey and Jasmine walked through the front door, despite Poppy's best efforts, everything descended into chaos.

Jasmine's waggy tail
knocked over a vase . . .

she frightened poor Flossy
with her barking . . .

destroyed one of mum's slippers . . .

and even caused trouble in the garden
when she started digging up the flowers . . .

Just when Poppy thought things couldn't get any worse, Jasmine dashed back into the house, through the kitchen, the hall and the sitting room, and into Poppy's bedroom.

"Jasmine, come back, you naughty girl," called Poppy.

"Oh, no!" said Honey when they finally caught up with her. "Look what she's done!"

Poppy came over to where Honey was and noticed a little puddle on
the floor in the corner of her bedroom.

"Quick, pass me the tissues!" said Poppy. "We need to clear this up.
I'll never be allowed to keep her if Mum and Dad find out."

When Mrs Meadowsweet came to collect Jasmine that afternoon, Poppy could hardly bear to say goodbye. She was quite sure that Mum and Dad would never agree to keep the puppy now.

She gave Jasmine one last hug.

Poppy felt very sad. All her dreams of having a puppy were shattered.

She went to bed that night feeling very sorry for herself . . .

But the next morning Poppy
woke up with a start . . .

It was Jasmine jumping on her bed!

At first Poppy thought she must be
dreaming, but she knew it was real
when she saw Mum and Dad.

"Surprise!" they chorused.

"Wow!" gasped Poppy. "Can I *really*
keep her?"

"So long as she stays away from
slippers, vases and flowers, and you
clear up all her little accidents!"
laughed Dad.

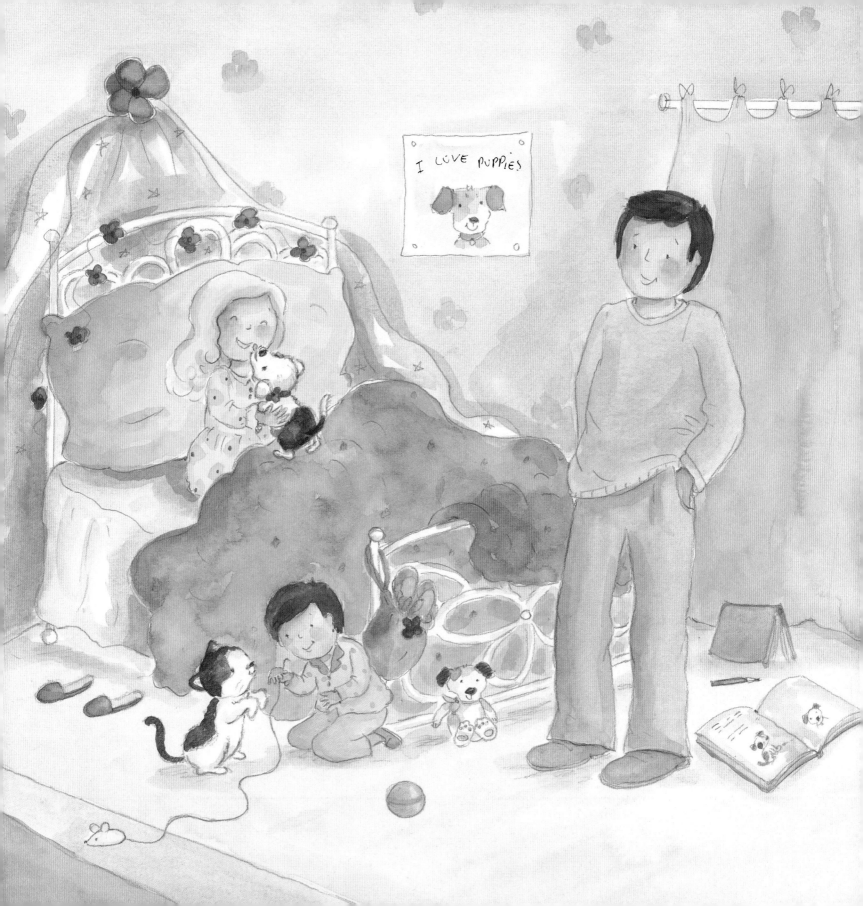

"You've impressed us with the way you've looked after Jasmine. You're such a devoted little princess!" explained Mum. "And she's adorable – how could we let her go to another family?"

"Thank you!" smiled Poppy. She felt like the luckiest princess in the world.